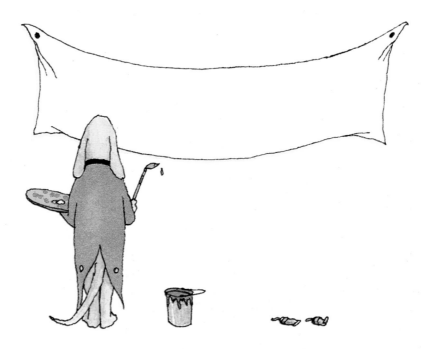

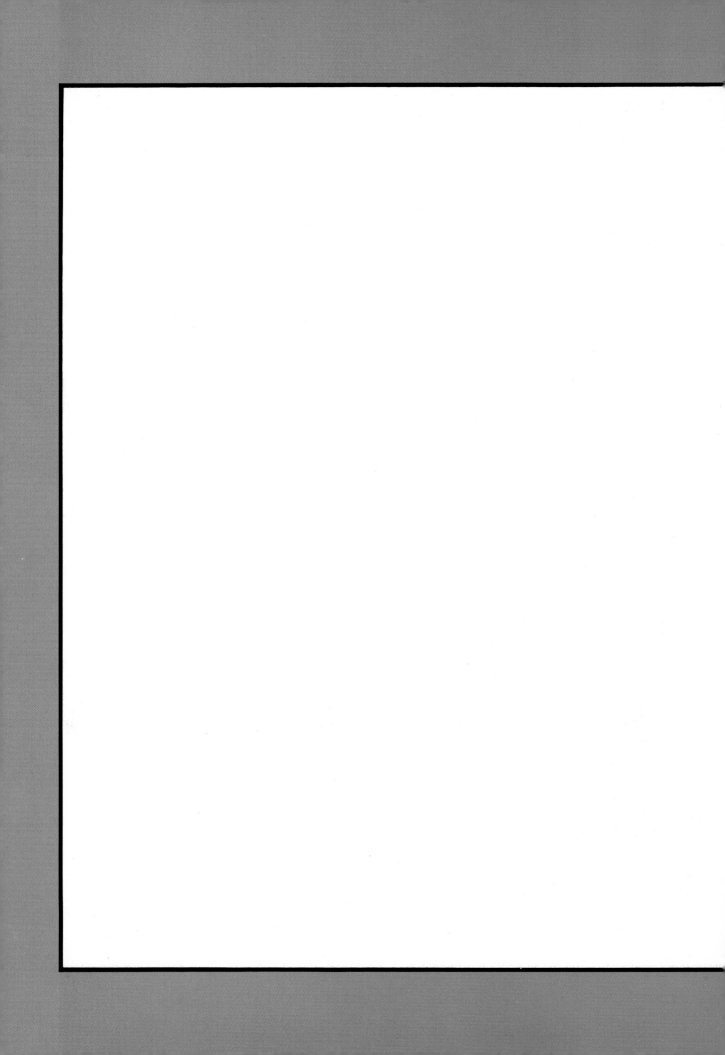

Story and Pictures by John Stadler

ALADDIN BOOKS
an imprint of Macmillan Publishing Company
866 Third Avenue, New York, NY 10022
Collier Macmillan Canada, Inc.

Animal Cafe is also published in a hardcover edition by Bradbury Press

First Aladdin Edition 1986

Printed in Italy

Library of Congress Cataloging-in-Publication Data
Stadler, John.
    Animal cafe.
    (Reading rainbow book)
    Summary: Old Max never suspects the true source of his shop's financial success.
    [1. Restaurants, lunch rooms, etc. — Fiction.
2. Animals — Fiction]   I. Title.   II. Series.
[PZ7.S77575An 1986]   [E]   85-26789
ISBN 0-689-71063-1 (pbk.)

To Al Manso

$\mathbf{M}$axwell owned a food shop. Sometimes business was good and sometimes business was bad.

But good or bad, it was all the same to Maxwell, for one morning each week he found that the foods on his shelves had vanished overnight and his cash register was stuffed full of money.

"Must be magic," he said.

As Maxwell closed the shop one Friday evening, he said to his cat and dog:

"You, Casey, you're such a lazy cat you couldn't catch a mouse if it were sitting on top of your nose. And you, Sedgewick, some watchdog you are! A burglar with bells on his feet wouldn't keep you from snoring. Sleep! Sleep! Sleep! All you do is sleep."

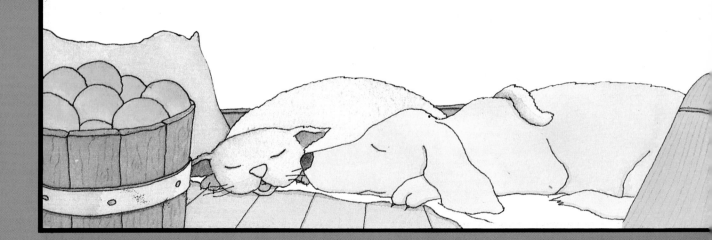

"Sweet dreams," Maxwell whispered as he left the shop.

In a flash Sedgewick and Casey were up and about. "All clear!" Sedgewick called from the doorway.

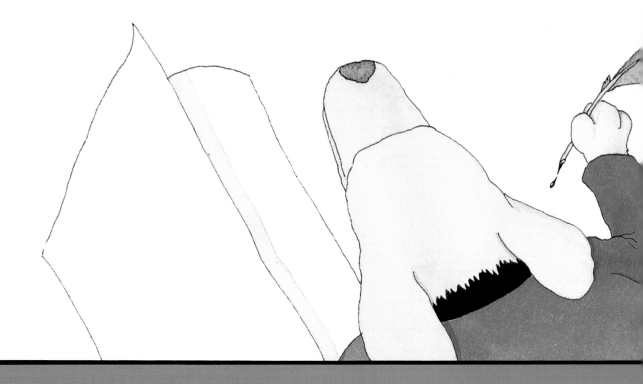

Casey was already in the kitchen slicing, dicing and spicing.

"What are you cooking tonight?" Sedgewick asked. "I'm writing out the menus."

"It's an old family recipe – a tasty dish of chipped beef with a touch of cheddar cheese, some chopped liver and lima beans, with some spinach, garlic and prune juice tossed in for good measure."

"Fine. We'd better call it Casey's Combustible Casserole," Sedgewick said.

Then Sedgewick ran from place to place decorating the shop.

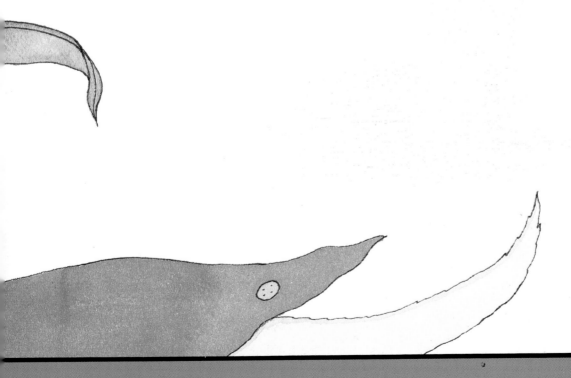

From outside Casey and Sedgewick heard the sound of approaching footsteps and chattering voices. Someone pounded on the door.

"Just in time," Casey cheered.

"Welcome back, friends," Sedgewick said as he opened the door to the first guests.

"Delighted, I'm sure," answered Mrs. O'Hare.

"Wouldn't miss it for the world," added her husband.

"Uh, oh!" Casey whispered. "Here comes Cutlet! Last time he ate us out of house and home. And then he complained about the meal being pork 'n' beans."

"Just be nice," Sedgewick said through a stiff smile. "Well, *hello* Cutlet. We were just talking about you. Welcome."

"Welcome, schmelcome," Cutlet snorted. "Where's the food?"

Soon many more guests arrived.

Professor Tuskanini of Huxley College was there, as well as Dr. Quackk. Lady Dumont was not far behind, accompanied by Colonel Kangaroo (retired).

All the guests mingled happily, discussing this and that.

"This," said one.

"That," said another.

Sedgewick saw that it was growing late and hurried the guests to their tables.

"What do you think of it?" Sedgewick asked after he served Casey's Combustible Casserole.

"It's – uh – well – I would say – er – undoubtedly
it's – uh . . ." replied Miss Goose.

The guests ate lightly, except for Cutlet who
constantly cried out for more.

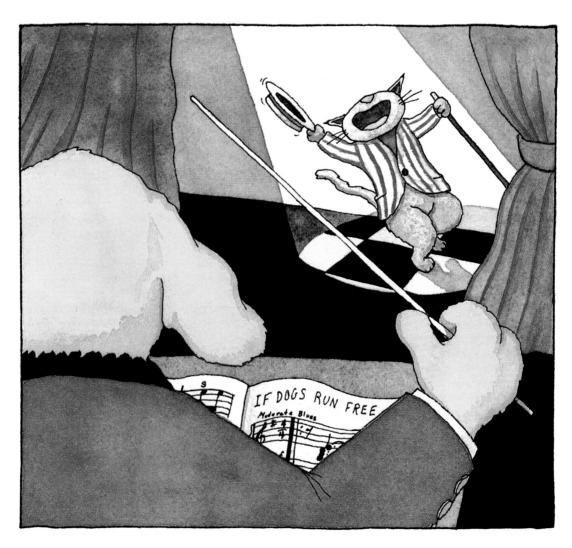

After dinner Sedgewick and Casey started the entertainment. First Casey juggled , and then he sang and danced. Then Sedgewick told jokes as Casey performed daredevil stunts. Finally they sang some old favorites together.

"Bravo!" roared Hubert the Bear.

"Mais oui!" cried Alicia La Gator as she got up to dance.

Suddenly Casey looked at the clock. "Yikes!" he yelled. "It's almost dawn. Maxwell will be back soon." The guests quickly lined up to pay their bills.

"Wonderful, wonderful," Lawrence Elk sang out.

"Oh, no," Casey shrieked as the last of the guests filed out. "Look!"

Cutlet was lying on the floor groaning.

"He's eaten too much again," Sedgewick complained. "We'll have to roll him out."

It was an enormous struggle.

Then Sedgewick and Casey rushed about to clean up the shop.

"Hurry," they yelled at each other, running in all directions at once. "Maxwell will be here any minute."

"I'm pooped," Casey whined as he scrubbed the dishes.

Sedgewick swept past him moaning, "Keep at it! He's coming..."

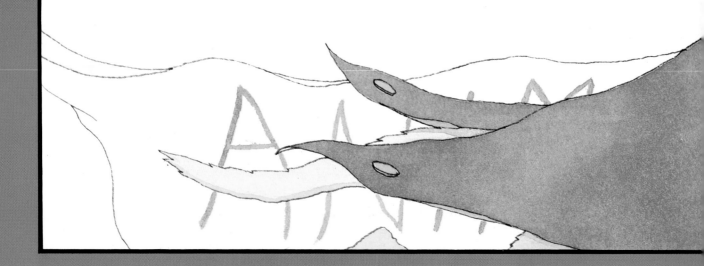

In a flash they finished the kitchen, washed up the shop, turned down the lights and locked all the money in the cash register. Just as Maxwell reached the door, Sedgewick and Casey dashed to the back of the shop, falling on top of each other in a heap.

Maxwell came in and turned on the lights. He opened the cash register and saw that it was full once again. And sure enough, his shelves were nearly bare.

"Must be magic!" he said.

Then he looked over at Sedgewick and Casey.

"Silly animals," he said. "All you ever do is sleep."

And that they did.

Behind the Scenes

un-To-Do Activities Begin on Page 48

Behind the Scenes

Introduction

The *Animal Cafe* only came alive after dark, but Sedgewick and Casey are not the only animals who work all night and sleep all day. Many animals keep the same hours. So do some humans.

Night Has A Thousand Eyes

Animals that are active during the night hours are called *nocturnal* (say: nock-**turn**-al). Their eyes are different than the eyes of day animals. Nocturnal animals can see in the dimmest light. Often their eyes are very big, which helps them gather in as much light as possible.

In the woods at night, the owl comes out to hunt. During the summer, frogs and insects are more active at night. And although you might not hear them or see them, the night forest is full of skunks, raccoons, opossums and porcupines. In winter, when food is scarce, deer come out during the day to find things to eat, but they prefer to look for food at night.

This change of shifts from day animals to night animals takes place in the desert too. The noises you're most likely to hear there at night are the howls and wails of the coyote. But the oddest night animal is the armadillo. It looks like it's wearing armor. The rattlesnake and the *gila* (say: **hee**-lah) monster usually hunt at night in the desert, too.

In the jungle, there are fewer nocturnal animals. However, jaguars and leopards are more active at night. Wild jungle pigs are too.

Bat Box

Bats are night creatures. They are misunderstood by almost everyone. Here are some common beliefs about bats, and the real story!

- Bats drink blood.

  TRUE — Some bats do, but most eat insects and fruit.

- The bite of a bat is deadly.

  FALSE — Animals can be bitten without becoming ill.

- The phrase "blind as a bat" is a good description.

  FALSE — The bat's eyes are good, but it does not use them to guide it in the dark. It "sees" with its ears which pick up sounds that bounce off nearby objects. This kind of "sound sight" is called *sonar*.

Behind the Scenes

- Bats like to fly into your hair.

  FALSE — Sometimes soft material like hair is not easily detected by the bat's sonar, but they do not purposely fly into hair.

- Bats live in caves.

  TRUE — Some do, while others live in barns, trees, and under bridges.

Eye-Dentification

Certain animals have something like mirrors in the backs of their eyes. This helps them catch any available light at night. If you should ever see creatures in the dark shining their brights at you, here's a way to identify what you're seeing.

Bright orange eyes, close together	Bear
Bright yellow eyes, low to the ground	Raccoon
Bright white eyes	Dog or fox
Yellowish white eyes	Bobcat
Bright white eyes, up in a tree	Porcupine

Animal Sleep

Have you ever watched a dog sleep? Every now and then its nose twitches. It may growl a bit. It's easy to see it's sound asleep, maybe even dreaming. But what about other animals? Do birds sleep? How about fish?

Every creature stops at least once during the day to rest. Some fish lie quietly on the bottom, others float on the surface. Butterflies hang on blades of grass, heads down. And rabbits doze in their nests many times during the day.

Can you imagine trying to sleep standing up? Many animals do. Birds wrap their claws around branches and sleep upright. They don't fall off because they have strong legs and feet to help hold themselves up. When the bird bends its knees, its legs and claws lock into place around the perch, and the bird cannot be moved off it.

Human Sleep

We must all sleep. In fact, we spend more time sleeping than doing anything else. A person sleeps for what amounts to about 25 years during a lifetime. That's almost one third of our lives!

What happens when you don't sleep? Do you become cranky? Do your thoughts become mixed up? Are you clumsy and slow? You must sleep in order to rest your body and refresh your mind. Sleep is so important to human beings that it is always being studied. People want to know how it works and why it's so necessary.

So far, we know that people need different amounts of sleep. Babies need to sleep between 14 and 18 hours a day. But as we grow older, our need for sleep goes down. An adult needs eight hours of sleep. Some can do well on less, while others need more. But eight hours of sleep is the average.

Just what happens during the eight hours you sleep? Do your thoughts turn off like a light bulb? No, they continue—but in a different way. Your night thoughts are not as sensible or easy to figure out as your day thoughts. And you have dreams. Another part of your brain takes over. What is your body doing during the night? It takes a rest. Your temperature falls one or two degrees, your muscles relax, and your breathing slows down. Your body is ready to start up full time once again in the morning after this break.

Dreamin'

Do you remember what you dreamed last night? Some people remember parts of their dreams. Others claim they never dream at all. Yet research shows that all of us dream four, five, even six times a night. How do we know?

In a laboratory, doctors watch people sleeping. When people dream, their eyes move rapidly. Doctors can see these eye movements. By counting the number of times these eye movements take place, a doctor can count the number of dreams that a person has had.

Other research tells us that all people dream in color. And that dreams are a way of thinking about what happens to you during the day. Do you usually remember your dreams? What kind of things do you dream about?

The Night Shift

Some people sleep during the day and work at night. Certain jobs simply need to get done while cities sleep. Think what would happen if you wanted to hear some news—and there was no one working at the radio station.

Behind the Scenes

- The baker makes bread and rolls for breakfast the next day.
- Newspaper workers put together the morning papers.
- Fruit and vegetable vendors set up stalls for their early morning customers.
- Post office staff sort mail for the next day's delivery.

The Man In The Moon, The People On The Moon

How can something we see every night of our lives be a mystery? Easily, if it's 250,000 miles away from us. That's how far away the moon is. It plays an important part in our lives and our imaginations — and it always has.

Long ago, people thought the moon was a god. It seemed alive. It changed before their eyes. From a fat, round moon, it would shrink to a tiny *crescent* (say: **kress**-ent). Then it would disappear, before beginning to grow round and fat once again. People prayed to the moon god and honored it with songs and dances.

Later, people noticed that the time between one full moon and the next full moon didn't change. They began to make a calendar based on the changes in the moon. Our word "month" comes from the time it takes the moon to make one cycle of changes—about thirty days.

Even while scientists were studying the moon, there were people who made up stories to explain its mysteries. Many of these stories are about a man in the moon. The shadows on a full moon can look like the eyes, nose and mouth of a face. Especially if you add a little imagination to the picture.

One of the stories from Germany tells us that the man in the moon is a villager who was caught stealing cabbages. He was sent to the moon, which looks a little like a large cabbage, as a nightly warning to others not to steal. When the sky is clear and the moon is full, can you spot the man in the moon?

Once telescopes were invented, we learned a lot more about the moon. For example, we now know that the moon doesn't have its own light. It shines with light reflected from the sun. And we know that what many scientists thought were seas on the moon are really large craters. A *crater* is a bowl-shaped pit on the moon's surface. The moon measures 2,160 miles across, which means that if it was placed on a map of the United States it would cover the whole center of the country.

Another important feature is the moon's gravity. *Gravity* is the force that holds us on the earth. Without it we would float away. The moon's gravity is 1/6th that of the earth. If you can jump two feet high on the earth, you would be able to jump twelve feet high on the moon. And if you weigh 90 pounds on earth, you'd only weigh 15 pounds on the moon. What a way to diet!

Until 1969, we had to study the moon from afar. But in that year Neil Armstrong and Buzz Aldrin, two American astronauts, landed on the moon. They became the first human beings to walk on it. They found two surprising things. First, although the moon looks smooth except for a few large craters, it turned out to be cratered everywhere. Large, small, deep, shallow, all kinds of craters. Second, the color was an even gray all over. The whole moon is the color of concrete.

From the beginning of time, people have been interested in the moon, our giant heavenly neighbor. Now we can visit there and get to know it better.

As Time Goes By

Did you ever hear a curious buzzing or beeping in a movie theater, a restaurant, or a supermarket? Did you know it was a watch alarm? People today rely on their watches not only to tell what time it is, but also to remind them of things to do. Simple time-telling is taken for granted. Any watch tells time, and almost everyone has a watch.

But telling time was not always so simple as putting a watch on your wrist or looking at the nearest clock. The earliest "clock" we had was the sun. People began to work when the sun rose at dawn. They stopped to eat when it was directly overhead at noon. And they stopped for the day when it sank below the horizon at sundown.

The time we tell is related to the sun's place in the sky. The ancient Egyptians used a sundial to tell time. A *sundial* is a flat disk with a raised marker. The hours are marked along the rim of the disk. In sunlight, the marker's shadow points out the hour as the day goes on and the sun moves across the sky. Of course, this kind of clock only works well on sunny days.

Next came the water clock, also an Egyptian invention. Hours were marked inside a big bucket or barrel. The bucket was filled with water and a small plug was removed from its botttom. As the water slowly dripped out, you could tell time by reading the mark showing inside the bucket. This clock worked well on cloudy and sunny days alike. Cold days were another matter—the water froze.

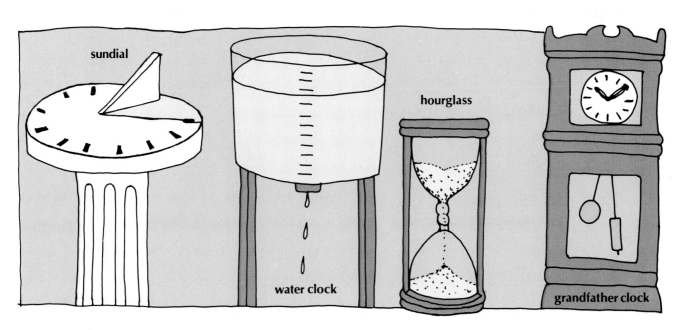

sundial

hourglass

water clock

grandfather clock

Behind the Scenes

What came next were sand clocks. Sand clocks used the same idea as water clocks. For example, an hourglass is designed so the sand takes exactly one hour to spill from top to bottom. The egg timer you may have in your kitchen is another kind of sand clock — it takes three minutes.

The first mechanical clock wasn't built until 500 years ago. Mechanical clocks used dropping weights to pull the pointer that showed the hour. These clocks put on great shows — one kind had a mechanical rooster that popped out and crowed every day at noon. Even though these clocks often didn't keep perfect time, people loved the entertainment.

The next big step in clocks was the *pendulum*. If you've ever seen a grandfather clock, you've seen the weight called a pendulum. It swings gently back and forth keeping the clock works going. In the 1920's, the pendulum was put aside in fine clock making. Quartz crystal clocks proved more accurate.

You might ask how watches fit into this story. They fit in as small clocks—originally with pendulums, now with quartz crystals. Why are they called watches? These small clocks were first used on ships, where sailors are on duty at different times of the day. Each time period is called a "standing watch," so small clocks have been called watches ever since.

Body Time

Sometimes we don't use clocks or watches to tell time. We use other signals. Sounds, sights, smells or feelings that come every day at the same time are body clocks. When your stomach growls, it's time to eat. When your eyes droop, it's time to sleep. And when you're feeling bouncy, it's time to go out and play. The smell of coffee is a morning smell to many people. An ice cream truck's bell means noon to others. Your neighbor's dog barking a greeting to its master tells you it's quitting time. What sights, smells, sounds and feelings do you use to tell time?

Hear Ye! Hear Ye!

Thanks to newspapers, radio and television, we get news daily. We know what's happening in our neighborhood, our city, our country, all over the world. There was a time long ago, however, when people heard news as much as a year after it happened—and even so, they thought it was *new* news. Nowadays, we get the news so fast, any news more than a few hours old is *old* news.

Long ago, it was easy to keep track of news in a village. You simply stopped at the town well, the general store, or anyplace people gathered and talked. When it was important to carry news about a river rising or a forest fire spreading, drum signals or smoke signals carried the news. Or people rode on horseback from one town to another, shouting the warning.

When news was important, but not a matter of life and death, the town crier would carry it. He would stand in the middle of town—or in several spots at different times around a large city—and shout the news. He would begin the news by ringing a loud bell and shouting "Hear ye, hear ye," as people gathered around to listen.

How do *you* find out what's going on? Do you listen to the news on the radio? Or watch the news on TV? Or read a newspaper?

What's Cooking?

What can you do when you get hungry in the middle of the night and your refrigerator is empty? Why not go to a diner for something to eat? This special kind of restaurant is open all day and all night. Diners serve fast, easy-to-fix food. Many people prefer diner food to fancy food. Neighborhood diners often serve the same customers — or diners (as in people who dine) — every day. They become friendly places to meet and greet as well as eat.

Diner cooks, waiters and waitresses have a special language of their own. At first, the words they use may not make sense. For example, "Adam and Eve on a raft" are code words for two poached eggs on toast. But once you know the language, or *lingo*, you can always tell what's happening on the cook's griddle. Here are some other examples of diner talk.

"Tube steaks" are hot dogs. "Cackler soup" is chicken soup and "red noise" is tomato soup. "Bossy stew" is beef stew and "sloppy joes" are ground beef in a spicy sauce. If you hear a waitress order a stack, you'll see pancakes being served.

Next time you eat at a diner, try out some of these phrases. You'll be surprised how easy it is to learn a new language when it's this much fun!

Activities ➡

Activities

Be A Weather Watcher

Keep your own record of the weather. Look at the chart on this page. Set up a chart like it. Then record the weather for several days. If you don't have an outdoor thermometer at home, you can find lots of daily weather information in the newspaper, and on radio and TV weather reports.

	Friday	Saturday	Sunday	Monday
Sunrise	6:32	6:32	6:33	6:33
Sunset	4:39	4:40	4:40	4:41
Temperatures				
8 AM	42°	40°	43°	39°
12 Noon	59°	60°	61°	59°
8 PM	42°	44°	40°	38°
Today Is:				
Rainy	✓			
Windy				✓
Snowing				
Sleeting				
Sunny			✓	

Trivia Game

Trivia are facts that may be unimportant but are very interesting. You can make up a game using trivia. Here are some to start you off. Put them on cards. Write the question on one side and the answer on the other. Stump your friends.

1. Q. Which president is on a penny, Washington or Lincoln?
   A. Lincoln. Washington is on a quarter.
2. Q. Which president's picture is on the dollar bill?
   A. George Washington
3. Q. American space travellers are called astronauts. What are Russian space travellers called?
   A. Cosmonauts.
4. Q. What animal swims like a fish, lays eggs like a duck and has fur like a mammal?
   A. The platypus, which lives along the banks of rivers and streams in Australia.

Make A Match

In *Animal Cafe*, Maxwell called Sedgewick and Casey lazy animals. But you know the animals were the opposite of *lazy*, they were very *busy*. Match each word with its opposite.

winter	full
sunrise	low
fat	summer
high	finish
empty	sunset
start	thin

Activities

Night Owls

Many people work while you are sleeping. Night workers are like the owls of the animal world — nocturnal. Each picture below stands for a group of people who work at night. Can you name each?

Word Search

Hidden in the maze below are words you've just read in the story. The words go across and down. Find the words in the maze and write them on another paper.

KITCHEN, MENU, SPINACH, MAGIC, ANIMALS, DAWN, CHEF, CASSEROLE, CHEESE, GUEST, KANGAROO,

L	E	S	O	G	U	E	S	T	E
M	R	P	N	I	T	L	D	D	L
A	K	I	T	C	H	E	N	I	C
G	S	N	W	R	M	I	E	M	H
I	C	A	S	S	E	R	O	L	E
C	T	C	M	X	N	E	E	C	E
L	E	H	W	R	U	B	C	H	S
A	Y	A	D	A	W	N	A	E	E
K	A	N	G	A	R	O	O	F	S
W	O	A	N	I	M	A	L	S	T

Activities

Hide And Seek

The chef is mixing a strange pot of stew. Can you find these objects: a boot, bow, butterfly, eyeglasses, glove and a key?

Mystery Objects

Read the clues and guess the mystery objects.

Object #1
1. It is very cold.
2. It might be flat or rounded.
3. Both kids and adults love to eat it.
4. It might have one stick or two.

Object #2
1. It smells good.
2. You use it several times a day.
3. It shrinks in water.
4. It chases dirt away.

Answers: 1. Popsicle 2. soap

52

Make Your Own Badge

Colonel Kangaroo wears a one-of-a-kind badge on his arm in *Animal Cafe*. If you could have a special badge, what would it look like? What would it tell other people about you? Here are some tips on how to make a badge you can wear. You must decide what it will look like. It might show your favorite sport, a special flower, or even your initial.

What You Need:
5″ square of heavy construction paper or felt scraps of cloth, or pictures cut from a magazine
large safety pin
tape
glue
scissors

What You Do:
1. Round off the corners of the 5″ square to make a circle.
2. Fringe or zigzag the edges of the circle.
3. Glue your initial or scraps of cloth or a picture to the circle.
4. Tape the safety pin to the back of the circle.

Activities

There is an unusual animal called a *liger*. It is half lion and half tiger. The first liger was born in a zoo in Salt Lake City, Utah, in 1948.

The difference between an alligator and a crocodile is in the snout. The alligator's snout is rounded. The crocodile's snout is longer and more pointed.

A real sponge that lives in the ocean is an animal. The sponge that you see and use is really the skeleton of the animal.

The word dinosaur means "terrible lizard." Dinosaurs belonged to the family of animals called reptiles. Snakes also belong to the reptile group.

Something Special

Make this special frothy drink for breakfast or for an afternoon treat.

What You Need:
6 oz. (¾ cup) milk or orange juice
1 egg
½ banana
a few strawberries

What You Do:
Combine all the food in a blender. Drink right away and enjoy!

P.S. Make a cool snack for later with the unused banana half. Cut the banana into slices. Coat with lemon juice so the banana won't turn brown. Wrap loosely in foil. Put in the freezer.

Activities

Make-It-Yourself News

Newspapers are filled with news and pictures, and it takes lots of people to put together each issue. But you can create your own newsletter for friends and family with some shortcuts and your imagination.

What You Need:
old magazines and newspapers
scissors
glue
pencil
ruler
blank paper
crayons

What You Do:
1. Plan three or four stories to include in your newsletter. Then, go through some old newspapers and magazines and look for words and pictures to use to tell your stories. For example, if you want to include a story about your birthday party, look for pictures of cakes, parties, balloons, presents and so on. And cut out words that have to do with parties, like "celebration" and "birthday" and "ice cream." You create sentences and headlines by piecing words together, combining all the words and phrases you cut out.

2. Next, figure out how much space each story will take. Using a ruler and pencil, outline *columns,* or areas to fit your stories.

3. Glue your headlines and pictures in place. Use crayons to add color to your newsletter.

4. Post your newsletter on a bulletin board, or pass it around so everyone can keep up to date.

Looking Back

How good is your memory? Can you answer these questions about *Animal Cafe*?

1. Who was the cook?

2. What color coat did Sedgewick wear?

3. Many animals came to the cafe. How many can you name?

4. What song did Casey sing?

5. Who told jokes?

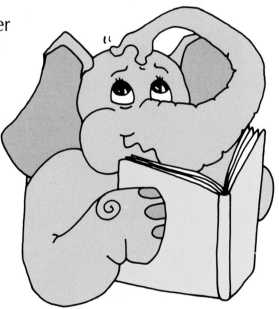

Answers: 1. Casey 2. Blue 3. The animals' names are: Casey, Sedgewick, Mrs. O'Hare, Cutlet, Professor Tuskanini; Dr. Quackk, Lady Dumont, Colonel Kangaroo, Miss Goose, Hubert the Bear, Alicia La Gator and Lawrence Elk. 4. "If Dogs Run Free" 5. Sedgewick

Activities

Jokes

"It's entertainment time!" said Sedgewick. "Have I got some jokes for you. Are you ready?"

What do cats put in their water to keep it cold?
Mice cubes.

Who is the largest mouse in the world?
E. Norm Mouse.
When is a black dog not a black dog?
When it's a greyhound.
What do you get when you cross a kitten with a lemon?
A sour puss.
How are a basketball player and a newborn puppy alike?
They both dribble.

Find An Animal

There's an animal hiding in each sentence. The name of the animal is split between two words. Can you find each name? The first name is marked for you.

1. Maxwell has one com(mon key)to open all doors.
2. Alicia La Gator says "I do go for you!"
    (*Hint: a four-legged animal that barks.*)
3. Cutlet is wearing yellow long pants.
    (*Hint: a night animal that is very wise.*)
4. Eaters wander in and out of the cafe.
    (*Hint: a large white animal that was once an ugly duckling.*)
5. The waiter walked over to a table.
    (*Hint: bird whose name rhymes with love.*)

2. (do go) 3. yellow long 4. eaters wander 5. walked over

Activities

Quiet Time

What do you do when there's nothing to do? Try this. Find a quiet spot. Sit under a tree or on the steps. Or you might lie on your bed. Then close your eyes and listen to the sounds around you. But first, read the poem on this page. Why not write a poem about what you hear!

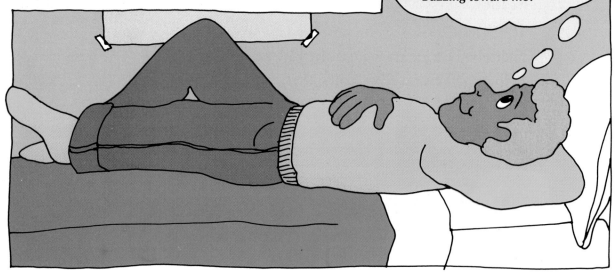

Ssh-h-h! Listen all around.
Check out every sound.
Snap, crack, bang, whizzz.
I wonder what that is?

Ssh-h-h! First it's high, then it's low.
It's a sound I don't know.
What can it be?
I'll wait and see.

Ssh-h-h! What do I hear?
A caterpillar crawling near?
A beetle or a bee
Buzzing toward me?

A Pair of Puppets

You can turn old socks into wonderful puppets. Just follow these steps to make "Harry" and "Whiskers." Ask an adult to help you.

What You Need:

2 large socks   buttons
tissues   scraps of felt
10 or 12 strands of yarn,   glue and pipe cleaners
    each 5″ long

What You Do:

Work on one sock puppet at a time.

1. Stuff one or two tissues into the toe of the sock.
2. Glue on buttons for the eyes and nose.
3. Glue on scraps of felt for fangs or a tongue.
4. Make a head of hair from the yarn. Tie the strands together by wrapping one strand around all in the middle. Make a large knot. Use a pipe cleaner to attach hair to sock. Trim the strands. Make some short, some long.
5. Make whiskers by sticking pipe cleaners through the sock around the nose.
6. Slip your hand inside the sock. Move your fingers up and down.

Activities

Plan A Puppet Show

Now that you have made your puppets, put on a show. First you must make up a conversation for Harry and Whiskers. They might tell a few jokes, too. Before showtime begins, make a stage with a bed sheet and an ironing board or a table. You can hide behind the sheet and the puppets will have a long stage on which to perform.

What's Your Order?

Step up and order a meal. Choose one item from each menu. You have $5.00 to spend. How many different meals can you order for five dollars or less?

MENU #1

fish chowder	75¢
frogs' legs	$1.00
buffalo stew	$1.50
acorn pie	$1.25
bug juice	75¢

MENU #2

egg roll	
lobster tail	50¢
dandelion salad	$2.50
peanut butter cookies	50¢
chocolate milk	$1.00
	75¢

MENU #3

banana soup	$1.00
Casey's casserole	$2.00
carrots & peas	50¢
ice cream supreme	75¢
ting-a-ling tea	75¢

Activities

Going Batty

Pictured below are some bats in flight and at rest. The pictures may look the same at first glance, but there are five differences. Can you spot all five?